Chester the Chipmunk

A Chesapeake Bay Adventure

This story was inspired by actual events.

Written by Cindy Freland

This book is dedicated to my beautiful daughters,

Alyssa and Andrea Bean

Thanks for all the encouragement, love and laughter.
I love you!

Chester the Chipmunk was three years old and he had so much energy. What was he supposed to do all day? He could eat sunflower seeds and corn-on-the-cob or play with Mister Big.

"Mister Big, will you please play with me?" asked Chester.

Mister Big was a huge, green, grumpy frog and didn't answer Chester. Mister Big just sat under the waterfall looking for bugs to eat.

Chester's home was near a pond. There were lots of fish, frogs, tadpoles, birds, butterflies, and blue dragonflies at that pond.

Since Mister Big didn't want to play, Chester thought about playing with the fish or he could run in and out of the rocks around Stump Pond. But that just scared the fish.

"Fish, will you please play with me?" asked Chester.

But the fish just swam in the pond and looked like shiny silver jewels under the water.

The fish and tadpoles shared the pond and they enjoyed eating bugs and moss from the yellow lilies.

Chester saw a little bird. "Little Bird, will you please play with me?" asked Chester.

It was Jasmine, the baby blue jay, and she looked hurt and scared. Chester wondered how he could help her.

"I will just stand close to keep you safe and warm," said Chester.

"That is very kind of you, Chester. I cannot find my mama. Do you know where she might be? I am very scared."

"No, I'm sorry Jasmine. I don't know where your mama is but I will help you look for her. Why are you hopping away from me Jasmine? Oh, you see your mama in the grass. Your mama will help you now. Bye for now, my blue jay friend."

Mister Big, the fish, and Jasmine wouldn't play with Chester. Then he had an idea. He decided to run to the other side of the pond to see his friend, Carly.

Carly was sitting on a tree that had fallen during the last storm.
"Hey, Carly, will you please play with me?"

"I would love to but I can't right now Chester because I have to find a
new nest. It was destroyed when this tree fell on it. There was also too
much water from the storm and it washed away all my food."

"I will help you find a new nest Carly."

"Thank you. I would like you to help me as I don't have any family or other friends nearby." Carly imagined how her nest might look.

"I will help you with your nest and help you find new friends. Merkle Wildlife Sanctuary is a wonderful place to live."

"Thank you Chester. It is very kind of you to help me."

"Let's run to the fence to see if there is a home for you. How is this spot?"

Carly and Chester were at the white, wooden fence which was there to guide the children walking on the trails. There were benches along the trail in case someone was hurt or needed to rest.

"This isn't a good spot because it is too noisy near the road and it is in the sun."

"We will look somewhere else. Let's run to the wood pile to see if there is a home for you. How is this spot?"

Carly and Chester were at the wood pile. The ranger chopped the wood to make a fire at special events. On summer nights, children gathered around the fire for story time and to make s'mores.

"This isn't a good spot because it is too damp under the wood pile."

"We will look somewhere else. Let's run to the pond to see if there is a home for you. How is this spot?"

Carly and Chester were at the pond and they saw lots of fish, frogs, tadpoles, birds, butterflies, and blue dragonflies.
"This isn't a good spot because it is too cold near the pond."

"We will look somewhere else. Let's run to my nest to see if there is a home for you, Carly. How is this spot?"

"At first I thought living near the pond might be too cold. But since you will be near too, it is the PERFECT spot. I will love living here!"

"Now that we found a new home for you, can we play, Carly?"

"Not yet. Now that we found the perfect home, we have to dig a new nest."

Carly and Chester dug a hole in the dirt near the pond for her new nest.

"Now that we dug a new nest for you, can we play, Carly?"

"Not yet. Now that we found the perfect home and dug a new nest, we have to find leaves to make it soft."

Carly and Chester went out to find leaves to bring back to the nest to make it soft.

"Now that we found leaves to make your nest soft, can we play, Carly?"

"Not yet. Now that we found the perfect home, dug a new nest, and found leaves to make it soft, we need to find food to last through the winter."

Carly and Chester went out to find food for her nest.

They looked near the pond and there was a birdfeeder with lots of sunflower seeds. They climbed the fence and hopped onto the birdfeeder. Then they gathered the seeds into their fat, little cheeks and scurried off to Carly's new nest.

After they gathered lots of sunflower seeds, Carly wanted to get other foods for her nest. So they looked around the pond to see what else they could find. They found a corn cob full of sweet kernels that was left in the trash from a picnic. So they nibbled the corn, filled their fat, little cheeks again and scurried off to Carly's nest.

Carly had over 5,000 sunflower seeds and corn kernels in her nest. Her nest was so full that she could hardly get into it.

"Can we play now, Carly? We found you a new home, dug a new nest, made it soft, and found lots of food for you."

"I would love to play with you now Chester."

"That's awesome! What should we do?"

"Let's check on Mister Big, Jasmine, and the fish."

"Look, Carly, there's Luther, the baby squirrel, taking a drink from the pond. We need to be very careful here, Carly. I heard there are…"

"WHAT'S THAT DARK SHADOW? YOWIE!"

"It's a hawk trying to pick up Luther and carry him off. We need to help him."

The hawk already had Luther in his talons.

"Carly, QUICK! Grab one of Luther's legs and I will grab the other one. Then maybe it will be too much weight for the hawk to carry."

But up, up, up they went, into the air. Then down, down, down, they all went into the pond. SPLASH! They were too heavy for the hawk after all.

Carly, Chester, and Luther swam across the pond and climbed on to the rocks after the hawk dropped them. Dripping wet, they ran for their lives as the hawk flew out of sight. Luther ran to his nest.

Carly and Chester hid in a hole until they calmed down. WHEW! That was scary!

After they calmed down from the fright of the hawk carrying them off, they visited Jasmine to be sure she was okay. Chester saw her under a tree with her mama. She was fine so Carly and Chester scurried away.

They visited the fish to be sure they were okay. The fish were eating mosquito larvae. They were fine so Carly and Chester scurried away.

They visited Mister Big to be sure he was okay. Mister Big was under the waterfall watching for bugs to eat. He was still grumpy but he was fine so Carly and Chester scurried away.

Carly and Chester never did play that day but they can always play tomorrow. What's important is that Chester helped three friends. He helped Jasmine find her mama. He helped Carly find a new home. He and Carly saved Luther from being carried off by a hawk.

It was a very good day on the Paw Paw Trail at Merkle Wildlife Sanctuary.

The Chesapeake Bay: A National Treasure

The Chesapeake Bay is 200 miles long, starting from Havre de Grace, Maryland, and ending at Norfolk, Virginia. It is the home for many animals, including, jellyfish, blue crabs, oysters, clams, striped bass, turtles, frogs, bald eagles, and ospreys.

The land around the bay, the watershed, covers seven jurisdictions, Delaware, Maryland, New York, Pennsylvania, Virginia, West Virginia, and Washington, D.C. The watershed is the home for many mammals, including beaver, bobcats, chipmunks, deer, foxes, rabbits, and raccoons.

FACTS ABOUT CHIPMUNKS, THE CHESAPEAKE BAY BRIDGE, AND THE BAY

1. The Chesapeake Bay Bridge opened in 1952, with a length of over four miles, it was the world's longest over-water steel structure at the time. The parallel span was added in 1973.
2. The bridge connects the rural Eastern Shore with the urban Western Shore of Maryland. Its average DAILY traffic is 61,000 cars.
3. The Chesapeake Bay is 200 miles from Havre de Grace, Maryland to Norfolk, Virginia. It is the home for many animals, including, jellyfish, blue crabs, oysters, clams, striped bass, turtles, frogs, bald eagles and ospreys.
4. More than 2,700 types of plants grow throughout the Chesapeake Bay watershed. Plants grow from forests to the shoreline and help keep the air and water clean. Plants also provide habitats for many mammals, birds and fish.
5. The largest source of pollution to the Bay comes from agricultural runoff, which contributes roughly 40 percent of the nitrogen.

6. Merkle Wildlife Sanctuary, located in Upper Marlboro, Maryland, is the only wildlife sanctuary operated by the Maryland Department of Natural Resources.

7. The sanctuary was named after Edgar Merkle (1900-1984), an active conservationist who devoted much of his life to protecting wildlife. He was known as the founder of Merkle Press in Washington, D.C. (1936).

8. The eastern chipmunk is a small, brownish, ground-dwelling squirrel. It is typically 5 to 6 inches long and weighs about 3 ounces.

9. The eastern chipmunk has two tan and five black stripes on its back, and two tan and two brown stripes on each side of its face. The tail is 3 to 4 inches long and hairy, but it is not bushy.

10. The chipmunk's range includes most of the eastern United States.

11. Chipmunks often create burrows in well-hidden areas near objects or buildings. The burrow entrance is usually about 2 inches in diameter. The chipmunk carries the dirt in its cheek pouches and scatters it away from the burrow, making the burrow entrance less conspicuous.

12. Chipmunks typically inhabit mature woodlands, but they also inhabit areas in and around suburban and rural homes.

13. Chipmunks enter a restless hibernation as winter approaches and are relatively inactive from late fall through winter months.

14. Chipmunks do not enter a deep hibernation but rely on the cache of food they have brought to their burrow. Some become active on warm, sunny days during the winter and most chipmunks emerge from hibernation in early March.

15. Chipmunks are considered minor agricultural pests throughout North America. When chipmunks are present in large numbers they can cause structural damage by burrowing under patios, stairs, retention walls or foundations.

16. Predators of the chipmunk include hawks, foxes, raccoons, weasels, snakes, bobcats, lynx and domestic cats. On average chipmunks live three or more years in the wild, but in captivity they may live as long as eight years.

17. Chipmunks are mainly active during the day, spending most of their day foraging. They prefer bulbs, seeds, fruits, nuts, green plants, mushrooms, insects, worms, and bird eggs. They transport food in pouches in their cheeks.

MORE BOOKS BY CINDY FRELAND

You will find books written by Cindy Freland on Amazon.com and www.cbaykidsbooks.com:

Jordan the Jellyfish: A Chesapeake Bay Adventure

Curtis the Crab: A Chesapeake Bay Adventure

Heather the Honey Bee: A Chesapeake Bay Adventure

Oakley the Oyster: A Chesapeake Bay Adventure

Olivia the Osprey: A Chesapeake Bay Adventure

Vandi the Garden Fairy

Lila the Ladybug: A Deep Creek Lake Adventure

Christmas with Marco: A Chesapeake Bay Adventure

Author:
Cindy Freland

Cindy Freland's inspiration comes from her love of children and animals. Most of her children's books are based on true events. Her passion is teaching children about the Chesapeake Bay. She worked at a major health insurance company in Washington, D.C. for 25 years. Freland started a business in 1997 and has continued managing it for 20 years. She is a Teacher's Aide at a private school. You can find her books on www.amazon.com and www.cbaykidsbooks.com. Freland lives in Bowie, Maryland, with her family and dog, Juno.

Illustrator: Javier Duarte

Javier Duarte is a Uruguayan illustrator born in Montevideo in 1979. In 1993 he began studying graphic advertisement at Pedro Figari School of Fine Arts. In 2002 he began a new and extensive career at Continental Art School with Professor Alvaro Fontana successfully passing the regular course of art and artistic workshops extension (ART TRAINING SYSTEM) until 2013. He's specialized professionally in illustration, portraits, cartoons, comics, storyboards and illustrating children's books (published in USA) and is currently working as a freelance locally and internationally. Contact information: Art of J. Duarte on Facebook at https://www.facebook.com/artofjduarte or by email at javierdgarces@yahoo.com.ar.

CPSIA information can be obtained at www.ICGtesting.com
Printed in the USA
BVIW121600141219
566259BV00002B/11